The Best Day of the Week

Written by
HANNAH COLE

Illustrated by
JOHN PRATER

WALKER BOOKS
AND SUBSIDIARIES
LONDON • BOSTON • SYDNEY

For Corin

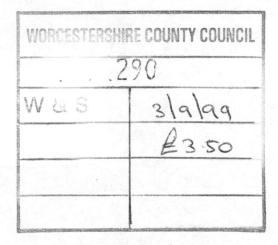

First published 1997 by
Walker Books Ltd, 87 Vauxhall Walk
London SE11 5HJ

This edition published 1997

2 4 6 8 10 9 7 5 3 1

Text © 1997 Hannah Cole
Illustrations © 1997 John Prater

This book has been typeset in Plantin Light.

Printed in England

British Library Cataloguing in Publication Data
A catalogue record for this book is
available from the British Library.

ISBN 0-7445-5467-5

CONTENTS

Grandpa put Fergus up in the plum tree
to frighten off the birds.

Saturday was the best day of the week. It was the day that Carole and Angela spent at Granny and Grandpa's house, while Mum went to work. Fergus always went too. Fergus was Angela's bear.

Granny pulled out the sofa so that Angela could make a house behind it for Fergus.

Grandpa put Fergus up in the plum tree to frighten off the birds that came to eat the buds.

When one of Fergus's legs came off, Grandpa found some very strong thread and Granny sewed the leg back on while Grandpa read a story to take everyone's mind off the operation.

This Saturday, it was raining and raining. It had rained all yesterday and all last night. The sky was dark and the roads were shiny.

"You'd better put Fergus in your bag," said Mum, "if he doesn't want to get soggy on the way there."

The way to Granny and Grandpa's house was along a road beside the river. There were houses on one side of the road, and water on the other side. The river was not very big, just wide enough for two boats to pass each other without crashing. Not many boats came along the river in winter.

"Why is the river so high up today?" Angela asked. Usually you had to look down to see whether there were any ducks waiting to be fed, but today the water was nearly up to the pavement. It was gushing along, bubbling and swirling. It looked very dark.

"I didn't realize there was such a flood," said Mum.

"It's not a flood," said Carole. "It's just a full river. All this water will go down to the sea, won't it? It always does."

"I hope the river doesn't get any fuller," said Mum, "or it will be over the edge and into the road."

They turned down a road away from the river and into Granny and Grandpa's street. The river was out of sight now. Rainwater was rushing along the gutters at either side of the road and gurgling down the drains. The gutters looked like little streams.

"If the river does overflow," Angela asked, "can't all the water just go down the drains?"

"They'll get full up," said Carole.

There were steps up to each front door in Granny and Grandpa's street. Angela ran up them and jumped down again.

"Hurry up," said Carole. "We're getting wet. You don't have to jump off all the steps."

Angela jumped off another set of steps.

"You splashed me," said Carole.

The pavement was so wet that you couldn't jump without making a splash.

"Let's cross the road," said Mum.

"Just let me jump off Sheila's steps," said Angela. Sheila lived opposite Granny and Grandpa's house. Angela ran up her four steps and jumped down. Sheila opened the front door.

"Hello, jumping bean," she said. "How high was the river when you came by?"

Angela put her hand down on the pavement. "Nearly this high," she said.

"That's a bit too high," said Sheila. "I don't know why the Council don't just put it all in bottles and keep it out of mischief."

"Come on!" Carole shouted. "We're crossing over!"

Granny opened her door and waved to Sheila.

"Wretched rain," she said. "Come on in and get your wet things off."

She took off their boots as they stepped in. She always did that. Her floors were very clean. Angela took her coat off and ran to the back window. The garden looked very wet.

Mum didn't come indoors. She was going straight on to work. "I didn't realize the river was so high," she said. "Are you worried about getting flooded?"

"We should be all right even if the roads flood," said Granny. "The water would have to come right up these steps before it reached the front door."

"Listen," Mum said to Carole and Angela.

"Granny and Grandpa are going to be worried about the flood. You two must promise to be good."

"I'm always good," said Angela.

"Nobody's *always* good," said Carole. "Specially not you."

Mum set off for work.

Usually Carole and Angela had a second breakfast as soon as they arrived, because their first one had been so rushed. But today Grandpa came downstairs and said, "Two helpers. Good."

"We're taking everything upstairs," Granny said. "Just in case." She disappeared upstairs, carrying the hoover.

"Just in case what?" Angela asked.

"In case the river gets higher and higher," said Carole, "and great waves come rolling down the road, and the water splashes the door down and fills up the house."

Angela took Fergus out of her rucksack and hugged him.

"Don't worry," said Grandpa. "If the river does get higher, there won't be waves. It will just slop over the edge, and trickle down the road. And if quite a lot of water trickles along here, it might seep under the crack at the bottom of the front door, and make a puddle on the floor. We'd be quite safe upstairs until the water went away again."

That didn't sound so bad.

"Is the rain easing off at all?" Granny asked.

Angela looked out of the window.

"It's still splashing up out of the puddles," she said.

"Let's get everything upstairs," said Granny.

"Everything?" said Angela. The kitchen was full of things. "Even the cupboards?"

"Not the cupboards," said Carole. "They're fixed to the floor."

Granny asked Carole to fill a cardboard box with the saucepans from the cupboard next to the cooker.

"We don't want them to get muddy if the water does come in," she said.

"The water is very muddy," said Angela. "It was all brown today."

"That's because it's been rushing along, washing away new bits of the riverbank that don't usually get washed. Angela, could you put all the toys in this box?"

Angela opened the toy cupboard in the living-room. There were games and puzzles that had been Mum's when she was little, and a few things from when Granny and Grandpa were children. Carole and Angela played with them when they came to visit. Angela began to take them all out.

"I've found the circus puzzle!" she shouted. "I thought it was lost!"

Carole came in from the kitchen. "We're not doing puzzles now," she whispered. "We're helping Granny and Grandpa."

"I wasn't doing it," said Angela. "Only finding it."

She put all the puzzles at the bottom of the box. There was a little green tin at the back of the cupboard that she had never noticed before. The lid was stuck.

"What's this?" she asked Granny.

"I can't remember," Granny said. "Let's have a look later, when everything is safely upstairs."

Angela filled the box, and put the green tin in last. It rattled. She put Fergus on top, and Grandpa carried the box upstairs.

When she had unloaded the toys upstairs, Angela took Fergus down in the empty box and helped to fill it with books. Grandpa carried the books up, and Granny took up the bookcase, with Fergus lying on the top shelf.

"You shouldn't make Granny and Grandpa carry Fergus up every time," Carole said. "It makes extra work for them."

"That little teddy doesn't weigh a feather," said Grandpa. "He can come for the ride if he wants to."

He gave them other boxes to fill. In the middle of the loading and unloading, they had sandwiches for lunch. Everyone was too busy for real cooking. They looked out and saw that the gutters at the sides of the road were full of dark river-water, not gushing along to gurgle down the drain now, but lying still as a pond, except for the rainwater splattering into them.

"It looks as though the river's come over

the bank," said Grandpa.

Granny rolled up the living-room carpet. The room looked very bare without it.

"Shall we take the chairs upstairs, Grandpa?" Angela asked.

"You could take that little stool," said Grandpa, "and Carole, could you carry up this lamp, very carefully?"

Angela gave Fergus a ride on the stool, and wondered what was in the green tin.

Grandpa carried the television up.

"I've always wanted to watch it in bed," he said.

The downstairs rooms got emptier and emptier. The rooms upstairs were so full you could hardly move in them.

When they looked out of the window again, there was no road and no pavement, just water stretching across to Sheila's house. She was standing in her window, looking sadly out at the flood. Angela could see the reflection of Sheila's house upside-down in the water.

Carole and Angela took the tins and packets out of the food cupboard. Angela made a tower of baked bean tins.

"That's not very helpful," said Carole.

"We'd better take the sofa up," Angela said. "It will get all soggy, like when I spilt my drink on it."

"The stairs aren't wide enough," said Carole.

"The cushions needn't get wet," said Granny. "Could you take one each?"

The sofa looked very uncomfortable with no cushions on it.

"Let's stand it up on some bricks," said Grandpa. "That might just be enough to keep it dry, if the water isn't very deep."

Granny fetched some bricks.

"The water's starting to come into the garden," she said.

She and Grandpa held the sofa up off the ground, while Carole pushed a brick under each corner. Then they did the same with the fridge.

"I think that's all we can do for now," Granny said. "We've done well."

Angela took Fergus to the window, to see the flooded road.

"It's stopped raining!" she shouted. "We can bring everything downstairs again!"

"Oh, I am glad it's stopped," said Granny. "But I'm afraid the water won't go down straight away. The river is still rushing along, and the rainwater that fell this morning is still trickling off the land into the river. So we may yet get flooded."

Angela looked out of the back window. The garden was a giant paddling-pool. The plum tree stuck up out of the water.

"Is this house an island?" Angela asked.

"Of course not," said Carole. "It's got houses stuck to it on both sides. Islands have water all round them."

It felt like an island, with water up to the walls, whichever window you looked out of.

Granny leaned out of the kitchen window, and looked at the front door.

"It's up over the bottom step," she said. "Oh dear, I don't want it to come in. It was dreadful last time, with all that mud. We had to scrub it off, and repaint everything. And the smell stayed for weeks. Months. Oh dear."

Angela hugged Granny.

"It won't come in, Granny," she said. "It won't."

"We'd better keep busy," said Granny. "It's no good sitting and watching the water coming up. What shall we do?"

"Let's see what's in that little tin," said Angela.

"Don't bother Granny with little tins," said Carole. "She's much too worried."

"A little tin sounds like a good idea," said Grandpa. "I wonder what it is? Run and fetch it, Angela."

So Angela ran upstairs for the tin. Granny managed to pull the lid off.

"Chalk," she said.

Angela looked at the sticks of white chalk, none of them quite new. She had hoped for something more interesting.

"What do you use chalk for?" Carole asked.

"Hopscotch, of course," said Granny.

Carole and Angela looked at her.

"Sam," Granny said. "I don't think these children know what hopscotch is."

"We'd better show them," said Grandpa, "when the garden's dried out. Fancy not knowing what hopscotch is."

"I think we'd better show them right away," said Granny.

"In here?" said Grandpa, looking round at the bare, clean living-room floor.

"If the water comes in," Granny said, "it will wash the chalk off, and if the water doesn't come in, I'll be very happy that there's only chalk to clean up."

"I think she's going to draw on the floor," Angela whispered to Carole.

Granny drew a pattern of big squares on the floor, with numbers in them.

"What can we throw?" she asked.

Grandpa fetched a dried bean from the kitchen. Granny stood at one end of the hopscotch pattern, and threw the bean into the square marked number one. Then she jumped across on to the next square, and hopped and jumped to the end of the pattern. She turned round and jumped and hopped back again, and picked up the bean.

"You have to throw it on to the number two square next," she said. "Then three. The throwing gets harder as you go on. And you mustn't step on the lines."

Carole had a turn. Angela wasn't very good at hopping, so Grandpa held her hand. Grandpa had a turn, and hopped on a line.

"You're out!" said Granny.

"Don't make him be out," said Angela. "He's got very big feet."

"All right," said Granny. "One more try."

While they played, Angela had forgotten about the flood. Now she saw Granny looking out of the back window. She looked out too.

"The plum tree has shrunk," Angela said.

Granny was very good at hopscotch.

"It was much taller than that."

"Trees don't shrink," said Carole. "The water has come up, that's all. Whose turn is it?"

Granny was very good at hopscotch. She threw the bean into each square and never missed. She hopped over it, back to it, and picked it up, without ever stepping on a line. Grandpa was good at throwing the bean into the right square. Carole was quite good at it. Angela hardly ever got it into the square that she was aiming at.

"Don't throw it so hard," said Carole, when the bean skidded right across the room.

"Throw it harder," she said, when the bean dropped on to the floor just by Angela's feet.

Angela couldn't get it right. Granny offered to throw the bean for her. Grandpa said she could carry on hopping even if her bean hadn't gone in the right square.

"You can cheat if you like," said Carole kindly, but Angela just sat down and watched the others.

"Where can I draw a special hopscotch for Angela?" said Grandpa.

Granny's big squares had taken up all the middle of the living-room floor.

Grandpa took the chalk to the kitchen and drew a smaller set of squares for Angela.

"Just up to six," he said. "That's enough for a beginner. Now, I know you're good at throwing the bean into the one square. You practise hard until you can get it into the two and three squares just as well."

He got her a bean from the jar. Angela practised and practised. She found that there was a good way of throwing the bean, rolling it along the floor. She got better at knowing how hard to roll it.

"There's Sheila looking out of her window," said Grandpa. Grandpa opened his front window.

"Isn't it terrible!" he shouted across the flooded road.

"It's still coming up," Sheila called.

"We'll need a boat," Grandpa shouted back. He was joking, but he didn't sound very happy.

He shut the window again, because it was cold.

Granny and Carole had heard the shouting. They came to wave to Sheila, and look out at the water. It felt as though the water was less likely to come right up to the front door if they kept an eye on it. Two of Sheila's front-door steps were still above water.

"Move over, Angela," Carole said.

"You're squashing me."

"Mind Granny's toes," said Grandpa.

"Don't fidget, Angela," said Carole.

Angela went back to her hopscotch. She had got much better at throwing the bean. She decided to try the whole game, all the way up to six. She threw the bean on to one, and hopped to the end and back. She threw it on to two, and hopped to the end and back. She threw it on to three. She kept on throwing and hopping. When she got to six, the bean jumped out of her hand too fast, and went out of the square.

"I nearly did it!" she said. "The bean just wouldn't go in the six."

"Be quiet," said Carole, by the window. "We're busy worrying about the flood."

Angela tried again. She threw the bean on to one, and on to two, and on to three. She hopped very carefully. When it came to six, she told the bean that it had to go into the six square, and it did. She hopped into one, jumped into two and three, hopped into four, hopped on to five, picked up the bean, turned round and hopped all the way back.

"I did it all the way up to six!" she said.

But no one was listening.

Grandpa had the window open again, and was peering round at their front-door steps. "I think the water's gone down a bit," he said.

"It looks just the same to me," said Granny.

"Was it up to that line on the lamp-post before?" Carole asked.

Angela went to look out of the window.

"Don't push," said Carole.

"Mind my toes," said Granny.

"It has gone down," Angela said.

"Do you think so?" said Grandpa.

"You don't really know," said Carole.

"I do," said Angela. "Sheila's got two and a half steps now. She only had two before."

"I can't bear to watch it," said Granny. "Let's go and have one more game of hopscotch, and then we'll come back and see how Sheila's steps are getting on. She definitely has two and a half now."

They went into the living-room and played hopscotch again.

"You're better than me now," Carole told Angela.

When they had all had a turn, they went back to the front window.

"Sheila's got three steps now," said Angela.

Granny opened the window and peered out at their own steps.

"You're right, Angela," she said. "It really is going down. Thank goodness, we're not going to be flooded this time."

"We'd better celebrate," said Grandpa. "Carole, see if you can find anything nice upstairs."

"I saw some chocolate biscuits," said Carole.

"Good idea," said Grandpa.

Carole fetched the packet of chocolate biscuits from the bedroom.

"There's Sheila," said Granny.

"She'd better have a biscuit too," said Grandpa.

"Can you throw it that far?" said Angela.

"Granny's the expert at throwing," said Grandpa.

So Granny threw a chocolate biscuit into Sheila's window across the rivery road. It broke in two as she tried to catch it, but she didn't mind.

"We needn't have bothered taking

31

everything upstairs," Sheila called across. "Still, with the downstairs rooms all empty, I suppose we can have a good spring-clean."

"Not us," Granny shouted back. "We're busy playing hopscotch."

PANCAKE DAY

Grandpa always made a cake for Carole and Angela when they visited.

"Isn't it time for that cake of yours, Sam?" Granny would say.

Carole fetched plates, and Grandpa made Granny a cup of tea. The cake was delicious.

"You're the best cook in the world," said Angela.

"Not as good as Granny," said Grandpa.

"Go on!" said Granny. "What can I cook better than you?"

"Fish pie," said Grandpa.

"Yuck," said Carole.

"And pancakes."

"I love pancakes!" said Angela. "Will you make us some, Granny?"

"It will be Pancake Day soon," Granny said. "We'll have pancakes next time you come. You can help mix them."

"Promise?" said Angela.

"Promise," said Granny.

But on the next Granny-and-Grandpa day, Granny wasn't there. She was ill, and in hospital.

"You don't want the girls today," Mum said to Grandpa. "I could take the day off work."

"But it's Saturday!" said Angela.

"Of course I want them," said Grandpa. "I'll take them to visit Granny in hospital. She won't want to miss seeing them."

They took Granny some daffodils, and Angela brought Fergus.

Granny was upstairs on Level Five. They

went up in the lift. Carole pressed the UP button to call the lift, and Angela helped Fergus to press the Level Five button inside the lift, to tell it where to take them.

Angela expected Granny to be in bed, but she was sitting up in a chair.

"You don't look ill," said Angela.

"The nurses take very good care of me," said Granny. "Hello, Fergus. It's nice to see you."

Angela tucked Fergus up in Granny's bed. It was a shame to waste such a high clean bed.

"Are you getting better?" Angela asked. "Will you be home in time for Pancake Day?"

"Of course she's getting better," said Carole. "That's what hospitals are for, silly." While Grandpa talked to Granny, Angela looked at the wheels under the bed, and the

Angela tucked Fergus up in Granny's bed.

curtain rails above it, and the locker next to it, where Granny kept her toothbrush, her reading-glasses and her books.

"It must be boring," said Carole, "in here all the time, with nothing to do."

"I sleep a lot," said Granny. "In fact, I think I'll have a nap now."

"Shall we go down in the lift then, Grandpa?" Angela said.

"You shouldn't sound as though you want to leave," said Carole.

"I don't want to leave," said Angela, "but I like the lift."

"It's been lovely to see you," said Granny. "Bring them again soon, Sam."

Grandpa wanted to talk to the nurses. "You go down and wait for me on the ground floor," he told Carole and Angela. "I'll be down in a minute."

The lift was already there, and Carole

pushed the Level One button.

"You've had more turns than me," said Angela.

"All right," said Carole. "You can push it to go up again."

"Then the lift will go up again," said Angela.

"We can go up in it," said Carole.

Angela pushed the button for Level Five, and Carole pushed the Level One button again.

"It's still not fair," said Angela. "You've pushed it more times than me."

"Push it again, then," said Carole. "Let's go right to the top."

The top button was for Level Ten. Fergus pushed it, and the lift went up. At Level Nine a nurse got in. She pressed the Level Three button, but the lift remembered that the Level Ten button had already been pressed, so it went up first, before it went down.

"What did you want on Level Ten?" the nurse asked.

"We wanted to come down again," said Angela.

"You mustn't play in the lift," said the nurse. "While you're making it go up and down, someone might be waiting for it, who needs it in a hurry for something important."

"Someone who's dying?" said Angela.

"Or someone rushing to make an ill person better," said Carole. "Are you rushing to make someone better?"

"Not this time," said the nurse. "I'm rushing to have my tea-break."

"That's quite important," said Angela.

"I think so," said the nurse.

The lift stopped on Level Three for the

nurse to get out. Then it went on down to Level One, and Carole and Angela got out. It had worked out fair with the buttons.

When Carole and Angela visited Grandpa next, they made cards for Granny. Carole wrote "Get well soon" in big letters on hers. Angela drew Granny tossing pancakes.

"You shouldn't go on about the pancakes," said Carole. "People who ask for treats don't get them."

They helped Grandpa in the garden. They stamped the vegetable patch flat.

"As flat as a pancake," said Angela.

"Angela," said Carole.

"Was that the phone?" said Grandpa, turning his ear towards the house. It wasn't.

They raked the flattened earth.

"That was the phone, I'm sure," Grandpa said.

"I heard it too," said Angela.

It was someone asking Grandpa to come to the hospital.

"We can take Granny's cards," said Angela. "Come on, Fergus."

The bus took them to the hospital. They hurried in and over to the lifts. Someone had already pressed the UP button.

"Can I push the button to Granny's level?" said Carole. "I'm the eldest."

"I'm the youngest," said Angela.

"Angela pushed it last," said Carole.

"Carole this time," said Grandpa. "Level Ten, Carole."

"Are you sure?" said Carole. But she pushed it.

"Has Granny moved?" said Angela.

"Yes," said Grandpa.

Level Ten looked different from Level Five, because the doors to all the wards were closed.

"This is the door," said Grandpa. "You'll have to wait outside. I brought some books for you to look at."

"Let's give Granny our cards," said Carole. "She'd like to see us."

"I'll take the cards," said Grandpa. "Wait here, and I'll be back in a minute."

They sat on chairs outside the door and read for a long time. Fergus did some acrobatics on the arm of Angela's chair.

"Is it a minute yet?" Angela asked.

"I think it's more than a minute," said Carole.

Sometimes the lift door opened and someone came out. Sometimes a nurse or a doctor or a porter went past. Angela was hungry.

At last Grandpa came out with a man in a white jacket. He was a nurse, called Brian. He was going for his lunch, and he would take Carole and Angela to the canteen with him.

"Thanks, Brian," Grandpa said.

"Grandpa didn't say goodbye," said Angela, when he had gone back through the door. "Why is he cross?"

"He's not cross," said Brian. "He's worried about your Granny."

"He looked cross," said Carole.

"He'll be cross with me if I don't get you some lunch quickly," said Brian. "I usually run down the stairs, for exercise, but as you're so hungry we'll go in the lift."

He took them down to the staff canteen on Level Three. He pushed the buttons, but Carole and Angela did not argue about it.

"What have they got for us today?" said Brian, looking at shelves of food. "They usually have some nice salads."

"Angela doesn't eat salad," said Carole.

"She's a fussy eater."

"Not *very* fussy," said Angela. "I eat ice-cream, and bananas."

"There might be pancakes," said Brian. "It was Pancake Day last Tuesday, and they've been doing them all week. Do you eat pancakes?"

"It can't have been Pancake Day yet," said Angela. "Granny said she would be at home to make pancakes for us on Pancake Day."

"We're doing our best to get her better," said Brian. "She'll make you pancakes when she gets home, I'm sure. But let's try these ones, even if they're not as good as your granny's."

They were good. They had two helpings. Fergus sat on the window-sill and watched them.

"My lunch-break's nearly over," said Brian. "We'll go and find your grandpa."

Fergus sat on the window-sill and watched them.

Grandpa was waiting for them outside the door to Granny's new ward.

"Shall we go home now?" Angela asked.

"Granny's very ill," said Grandpa. "I don't want to leave her. I've rung Mum, and she'll be here in a minute. Just wait here till she comes, there's good children."

He left them the books, but they had read enough for one day. They sat and watched the lift. Whenever the doors opened, they hoped Mum would step out, but it was always someone in uniform.

"Oh!" Angela said suddenly. She had remembered Fergus.

Carole looked at her.

"Where have you left him?" she said in a tired voice.

"I had him in the canteen," said Angela.

"You put him on the window-sill," said Carole. "You'd better go and fetch him."

"You come with me," said Angela.

"I'll have to stay here to explain to Mum when she comes," said Carole.

"Couldn't you get him for me?" said Angela.

"No," said Carole. "I'm reading."

"I can't," said Angela.

"All right," said Carole. "Don't."

"Mum might go with me when she comes," said Angela.

"She might," said Carole. "But she'll probably go in to see Granny, and she'll be worried like Grandpa, and she won't want to go down to the canteen just because of a teddy bear. She might say, wait till next time we come."

"Please get him for me," said Angela.

"Sshh," said Carole. She turned over a page.

Angela looked at the lift. She knew that the

canteen was on Level Three. She knew which was the canteen door, because you could see tables and chairs through the glass. If she wasn't quick, someone might notice Fergus on the window-sill and take him away.

She went and pressed the DOWN button by the lift door.

"Goodbye," she said.

"Goodbye," said Carole, without looking up from her book. But when the lift arrived and the door opened, she ran over and shouted "Good luck!" as the door slid shut again.

Angela pressed the button for Level Three. The lift began to go down. It was easy.

The lift stopped at Level Nine, and three doctors got in. At Level Eight, one doctor got out, and four nurses got in. At Level

Seven, two more doctors got in, and a porter with an empty wheelchair. Angela moved over to get out of its way. At Level Six so many people got in that she was pushed right to the back of the lift.

Now Angela couldn't see the numbers over the door that showed what level the lift had reached. She thought the next two stops must be Level Five and Level Four. At Level Four some people got out, but others got in, and Angela was still right at the back of the lift. Then, instead of going down, the lift began to go up. Angela could feel in her stomach that it was going up.

Afterwards, Carole said "You should have shouted, 'Stop! I have to get off!', and they would have let you escape", but in the lift Angela didn't think of that. If she had thought of it, she might not have dared to shout anyway.

When enough people got out for Angela to get near to the door, she pressed the button for Level Three, but the lift went on up. It didn't stop until it got right up to Level Eight. When the doors opened, Angela jumped out quickly. It was nowhere near the canteen, but Angela didn't dare go back in the lift again. The same thing might happen, and she might get stuck at the back of the lift for ever.

Brian had said you could run downstairs to the canteen. Angela searched for the stairs. She could not see them, but she could hear a hollow echoey sound of feet, and found a staircase winding down and down to where Fergus was waiting.

She ran down the wide white stairs past Level Seven, and Level Six, and Level Five, and Level Four, to Level Three.

She found the canteen easily. Fergus was

waiting patiently on the window-sill. Angela felt proud that she had managed to reach him, in spite of all those people blocking her way in the lift.

"We'll run up to Level Ten," she whispered into Fergus's soft ear. "And Mum will take us home. We won't tell anyone how I couldn't get to Level Three."

She found the stairs again, and ran up to Level Four. She walked up to Level Five. She walked slowly up to Level Six. She had to sit down to rest before she walked very slowly up to Level Seven.

"Not many more levels now, Fergus," said Angela.

At Level Seven they rested. At Level Eight they rested for a long time. But Angela began to worry that Mum would be waiting, or even that Mum and Carole might set off without her. She tried to run up to Level

Nine, but her legs were wobbly. The bones inside them had gone soft. She heaved herself up to Level Ten by pulling on the stair-rail.

At Level Ten she flopped on to one of the chairs outside Granny's ward.

"Mum's been here for ages," said Carole. "How did you take so long, just going down to Level Three and back?"

Angela couldn't say anything. She just sat and panted.

Mum came out through the ward door. She sat down with Angela on her lap, and put her arm round Carole.

"Shall we go home, Mum?" Carole asked.

"In a minute," said Mum. Angela wondered whether this was going to be another very long minute.

Then Mum told them that Granny had died.

"She might get better," said Angela.

"She won't," said Carole. "Once you're dead, you're dead, and that's that. Isn't it, Mum?"

"Yes," said Mum. "She won't get better, Angela."

"You're supposed to get better in hospital," said Angela. "That's what hospitals are for."

"The nurses and doctors worked very hard," said Mum. "But Granny was very ill. And she was old. People have to die when they are old."

"She wasn't too old to dig the garden," said Carole. "And play hopscotch, and make pancakes."

"I forgot the pancakes," said Angela. "She'll have to get better."

"Don't you understand?" said Carole. "She can't make pancakes now she's dead.

Can she, Mum?"

"Granny always keeps her promises," said Angela. "Brian's going to make her better, so she can make pancakes when she gets home. He said so."

"She would have kept her promise if she could," said Mum.

Then Angela knew that Granny wouldn't get better. Tears slid down her nose. They soaked into Fergus's furry head.

"She's only crying about the pancakes," said Carole. "I'm crying about Granny."

"It's the same thing," said Mum. "We're all going to miss the pancakes, and the hopscotch, and everything Granny used to do."

They all sat and felt sad together. Grandpa came out and sat down next to them. His face looked different from usual. Angela thought that he had been crying.

"I came to say goodbye," he said. "These girls have been so good."

"Why don't you come home with us, Grandpa?" said Carole.

"There are things to arrange," he said.

"They can wait," said Mum. "I'll tell the nurses we'll be back later on. Come home and have lunch. Or tea, or something."

"I'd rather be on my own for now," said Grandpa. "But come round tomorrow, will you?"

"Would you like to borrow Fergus for the night?" Angela asked. "To stop you feeling lonely?"

"I would," said Grandpa. "But I don't want him to feel homesick. Goodbye, and thank you both for waiting so patiently all day. And Angela?"

"Yes?"

"I thought we'd have Pancake Day

tomorrow. It will only be a few days late."

"Granny can't get better, you know, Grandpa."

"No," said Grandpa. "She can't. So I'll have to cook the pancakes. They may not be very good, but I can try."

"Can I help stir the mixture?" said Angela.

"Of course," said Grandpa.

"See you tomorrow, then," said Angela.

"See you tomorrow," said Grandpa.

They did make pancakes the next day. Grandpa found a recipe in an old brown book.

"Granny didn't need a recipe, did she?" said Angela. "She just tipped in the flour until it looked right."

They stirred hard, but the mixture went a bit lumpy.

"The lumps are quite nice," said Angela, when the pancakes were cooked.

"And it doesn't matter if pancakes stick to themselves and get holes in them," said Carole. "They taste just as good."

"We'll be better at them by next year," said Grandpa.

*Grandpa showed them how to play
cricket in the garden.*

The Pantomime Witch

Carole and Angela had always gone to
Granny and Grandpa's house on the day
that Mum went to work, but after Granny
died, Mum thought that she should stop
going to work on Saturdays. She thought
that looking after Carole and Angela would
be too much for Grandpa, now that he was
on his own.

"Oh no," said Grandpa. "I look forward to
my Saturdays."

Carole and Angela were relieved. It was
not the same without Granny, but it was still
the best day of the week.

Grandpa showed them how to play cricket
in the garden. By the time the summer

came, the garden was looking quite wild.

"What would Granny say about all these weeds?" said Carole.

"I think of them as wild flowers," said Grandpa. "Look, what could be prettier than this yellow one?"

"That's a dandelion," said Angela.

They took turns to hide Fergus among the wild flowers, and the others had to find him.

In the autumn, Grandpa decided to make new curtains for the living-room.

"Granny was going to make them in the spring," he said. "We bought the material, but then she got ill."

Grandpa let Carole and Angela turn the handle on the sewing machine. The curtains looked good. Grandpa made a tent out of the old ones and Angela and Fergus had their lunch inside it.

Winter came. Grandpa told Carole and

Angela that there was going to be a children's show at the theatre. It was called "Hansel and Gretel" and everyone could see from the posters that there was a witch in it.

Carole knew all about the theatre, because she had been to see a pantomime about Puss in Boots last year. But Angela had never seen a show. Carole told her all about it.

"There are hundreds of seats in straight lines," she said. "And you have to sit in the one with your number on it. You have to sit very still, and not kick the people in front of you. Then the lights go out, and the music begins, and you see the story happening on the stage. It isn't real, of course. It's only grown-ups pretending to be the people in the story."

"Will the witch be real?" Angela asked. "With a broomstick?"

"Well, of course she will have a

broomstick," said Carole. "But it will only be an ordinary person dressed up as a witch."

"But she will do real magic, won't she?" asked Angela.

"Oh, yes," said Carole. "Of course she will do real magic."

Grandpa bought three tickets for the show. He invited Carole and Angela to go to the theatre with him to see it on the next Saturday afternoon.

"Can I see the tickets?" said Angela. They were just three little scraps of paper with writing printed on them.

"These are good seats," said Grandpa. "They are in Row A, right at the very front of the upstairs balcony, so I think we will have about the best view in the whole theatre."

Carole and Angela had to put on their best

dresses to go to the theatre, and have their
hair brushed very hard. Angela didn't like
her best dress.

"You look lovely," said Grandpa.
"Everyone will think that you're the most
beautiful child at the theatre."

"Row A isn't very close to the stage, is it?"
Angela asked.

"Oh, quite close enough," said Grandpa.
"You will be able to see everything all right."

"But will everything be able to see me?"
asked Angela. "What about the witch?"

"No, no," said Grandpa. "The witch will
never notice you among all the hundreds
and hundreds of other children there."

But Angela rumpled her hair just in case,
so that she wouldn't show up too well by
being the most beautiful child at the theatre.

Angela wanted to take Fergus with her to
the theatre.

"Oh, no!" groaned Carole. "Not Fergus! Grandpa, she can't take that old teddy to the theatre! I'm not going with her if she takes it. Tell her she can't."

"Well, I don't see that it can do much harm if she does take him," said Grandpa. "He's such a little thing. He can't get in anyone's way."

So Fergus was allowed to go. If he hadn't been allowed to go, Angela wouldn't have gone. She put him in his best clothes.

The balcony was upstairs in the theatre. The stairs had purple carpets on them and golden handrails at the side.

"You don't have to jump up every step," said Carole. "You're supposed to walk properly in a theatre."

But they were such wide steps, with such soft carpet on them, that it was hard to walk properly on them. Angela jumped, and

Fergus slid up the handrail. Grandpa didn't mind.

They found Row A, and walked along until they came to their seats. Angela's seat was a very good one, red and furry. There was a shelf in front of it, but if Angela sat on the edge of her seat and leant forward, she could see the whole theatre. There were huge curtains hiding the stage, with large pillars on either side. Down below, on the floor of the theatre, there were rows and rows of seats. From up in Row A of the balcony, Angela could see right down on top of the heads of the people sitting down there.

"These are very good seats, aren't they, Grandpa?" said Carole.

"Lovely," said Grandpa. "We couldn't have a better view. Sit down, Angela, and don't lean over or I will have to hold on to you."

He had brought a bag of sweets and they all had one while they waited for the show to start.

At last the lights began to grow dim, and there was a sound of drums. Angela sat up very straight and held Fergus up on the shelf in front of her so that he could watch the curtains opening.

"Remember you have to be very quiet," whispered Carole to Angela.

"I am," Angela whispered back.

"And don't fidget," whispered Carole.

"I'm not," said Angela.

"Can't you put that silly teddy away?" said Carole.

"No," whispered Angela.

The show began. Hansel and Gretel were very poor. They lived in a cottage in the woods and they had hardly anything to eat. Angela knew the story already, and she felt very sorry for the two children on the stage. Every now and then she picked up Fergus and whispered into his ear, to explain the story. Then she put him back on the shelf.

When the witch flew on to the stage, everyone gasped. She was green all over, even her hair, and she looked terrible. She kept pointing at people with her bony green finger. Angela hoped that she wouldn't point at her or Fergus. She held Fergus tightly and covered his eyes so that he wouldn't be frightened.

"Don't be scared," whispered Grandpa. "Here, have another sweet."

Angela put Fergus down on the shelf for a minute while she unwrapped the sweet.

Suddenly Carole groaned. Angela looked at her in surprise. Carole had hidden her face in her arms.

"What's wrong with you?" Grandpa

asked. "Too many sweets already?"

Carole looked up. Her face was bright red.

"I told you not to let Angela bring that stupid teddy," she moaned, "and now she's dropped it over the edge. Oh, Grandpa, send Angela home. She's a disgrace to us all!"

Angela looked round in horror. Sure enough, Fergus was missing. He must have fallen right over the front of the balcony. Angela leaned over the shelf and looked down to the rows of seats below. The people down below were not watching the witch on the stage. They were all looking upwards, to see where the flying teddy had come from. But the whole theatre was dark, with only a faint green light coming from the witch's cauldron, and Angela could not see Fergus at all.

Then the people downstairs stopped

looking up, and turned back to the stage, so as not to miss the show.

"Sit down!" hissed someone behind Angela. "We can't see if you stand up."

Grandpa pulled Angela back into her seat. "Don't worry," he whispered. "We'll find your teddy after the show. Just sit back and enjoy yourself."

But Angela could not enjoy herself with Fergus missing. Supposing someone downstairs took a fancy to him, and slipped him into their own pocket? Then Angela would never see him again. Thinking about that made her cry.

"Tell her to stop sniffing," whispered Carole. "You're not supposed to sniff at the theatre."

Grandpa felt sorry for Angela. "It's all right," he whispered. "I'll go downstairs and find the teddy right away. You wave your hand when you see me, and then I'll know where you dropped him."

He got up and squeezed along to the end of the row and disappeared down the stairs.

The witch was still being horrible on the stage.

Angela peeped over the edge of the shelf. At last she saw Grandpa far below, looking rather lost in the darkness. She waved to him, and he waved back, and set off along the row of seats just below them. Now Angela knew that he would find Fergus, and everything would be all right. She began to watch the witch again.

"Ha-ha!" the witch was cackling. "I feel like a spot of magic! Now, what shall I do? Shall I turn you all into spiders?" she shouted, and pointed at all the children watching the show.

"No!" they all screamed.

"Shall I turn you all into toads?"

"No!"

The witch shook her nasty fingers and Angela could hear her fingernails clicking.

"I shall have to turn somebody into something," said the witch, "or I shall explode."

Suddenly she pointed at someone downstairs. "You, sir! I shall turn you into something! Come up here on to the stage, if you please!"

"I wonder who it is," whispered Carole. "Do you think she will really turn him into something?"

"I think she will," said Angela. "I hope it's somebody horrible, who deserves it."

But when the person got up on to the stage with the witch, and the green lights were shining on him, they could see who it was. It was not anyone horrible. It was

Grandpa, and he was holding Fergus.

"Look," said Carole. "He did find your silly teddy."

"But the witch is going to turn him into a toad!" said Angela. "Tell her to stop!"

"Stop talking," whispered Carole. "You aren't supposed to talk at the theatre."

Grandpa did not look frightened at all. He was laughing.

"Step into my cauldron, if you please," said the witch, and she picked up Grandpa's leg and put it into the cauldron.

"Ouch," said Grandpa. "It's boiling." Everyone could hear what he said quite clearly, because he was near the microphones on the stage.

"Now the other leg," said the witch. "Both feet in, double quick."

But the cauldron was too small for Grandpa to put both his feet in.

"Ouch," said Grandpa. "It's boiling."

"You're too big," said the witch. "Too big and too fat. I need someone smaller to work my wicked magic on." She looked around.

"Do you think she will let Grandpa go now?" whispered Angela.

"She might," said Carole.

Then the witch noticed Fergus in Grandpa's hand.

"Aha!" she hissed. "I see you have a cat with you. You must be a witch like me. Give me that cat and I shall turn it into a frog."

"He isn't a cat!" Angela shouted as loud as she could. "He's a bear, and you're not to turn him into anything, you horrible pig witch!"

"Sshh," said Carole. "You aren't supposed to be rude to the actors."

But with the cauldron crackling, and the band playing scary music, the witch did not hear Angela anyway. She snatched Fergus from Grandpa's hand and made some magic signs over him. Then she scattered some magic dust around him and walked in a circle.

Suddenly, in the witch's hand there wasn't a teddy any more, just a big green frog which hopped off her hand and vanished into the cauldron. This was the worst thing that had ever happened in the whole of Angela's life. It was too terrible even to make her cry. Grandpa was looking quite horrified as well.

"I wish Granny was here," Angela whispered. "She wouldn't have let the witch do that."

"Grandpa is too polite," Carole agreed. "You don't have to be polite to witches."

"I think you had better turn it back again, if you don't mind," Grandpa said to the witch. "That teddy belonged to my granddaughter, and she was very fond of it."

"I don't know about that," said the witch. "The magic may not work twice. We'll see. I shall need a little help. Will you help me?" she called out to everyone who was watching the show.

"Yes!" they all screamed back. Angela screamed the loudest of all.

"When I sprinkle the magic dust into the cauldron," said the witch, "you must say the magic spell as loud as you can. Split, splat, come back, cat!"

She sprinkled the magic dust, and everyone in the theatre shouted as loud as they could, "Split, splat, come back, cat!" except for Angela, who screamed, "Split, splat, come back, Fergus!"

The witch reached her bony green arm into the cauldron. Angela held her breath.

Grandpa was peering into the cauldron

and looking rather nervous.

"Supposing she has turned him into a cat?" said Angela. "I don't want a cat."

But it was all right. The witch pulled Fergus out of the cauldron and Grandpa snatched him back from her.

"Thank you," said Grandpa, and hurried off the stage.

The witch just carried on with her wicked spells while Angela waited for Grandpa to get back upstairs.

At last he arrived, out of breath from running up all the stairs. He gave Fergus to Angela.

"Oh, thank you, Grandpa," said Angela. "You were wonderful."

"Don't drop him again," said Grandpa. "I didn't expect to have to rescue him from a witch."

Angela kept Fergus on her lap after that,

and held him very tight. He looked quite all right. You would never have guessed that he had just been turned into a frog.

At last the show ended. Hansel and Gretel tricked the witch and turned her into gingerbread. Everyone clapped and cheered. Angela couldn't clap, because she did not dare let go of Fergus, but she cheered and cheered until Carole said, "You aren't really supposed to scream your head off at the theatre."

Fergus was sparkling with the magic dust that the witch had sprinkled over him. It stayed in his fur for weeks. Carole said it was only glitter, but anyone could see that it was magic.

THE

END

THE BEST DAY OF THE WEEK

Three affectionate stories about the special relationship between two sisters and their grandparents.

Hannah Cole read philosophy and psychology at King's College, Cambridge. Since then she has taught adults and children with learning difficulties. At the moment, she works mostly with autistic children. She is the author of a number of stories for young readers, including the popular football story, *Kick Off*. She has also written three novels for children, *In Between Times*, *In at the Shallow End* and *Bring In the Spring*. She lives near Oxford with her three children.